# Remembering Skyline

## Skyline Mountain Book 3

# LESIA FLYNN

*Remembering Skyline* Copyright © 2016 Lesia Flynn

Cover designed by Lesia Flynn

ISBN-10: 0990990842
ISBN-13: 978-0-9909908-4-0

*For Angela and Mac*

# ACKNOWLEDGMENTS

**Thank you, readers!** Your willingness to purchase and read my books is humbling. I appreciate each and every one of you. You are a vital part of my dream come true. If you enjoy reading my books, please take a moment to leave a review at any retailer. And by all means, please tell your reader friends about me, too! There is no greater thanks given to a writer than a review or a recommendation. Thank you all for that particular love!

A while back I found myself in a pickle. I had to make a quick trip to the grocery store and the only means of transportation was the truck my friends Angela and Mac rented while visiting me. When I tried to climb up into the truck, it became clear that I needed some assistance. Of course I did what any other short person would do, I retrieved my household stepstool! Imagine the surprise onlookers displayed when I had to step down into the parking lot (and back up again after shopping) in front of my small town grocery shoppers. Mac made a ceremonious show of it calling on her most well-mannered royal behavior. Not one of us had a camera but we will never forget that particular situation. This was the occasion that inspired a Dodge Ram in Ben and Cassidy's story. It was hilarious fun, much like any time the three of us are together. Thank you Angela and Mac. Without you, life would be boring and likely much more hazardous for me.

I would like to say thank you to Bambi Lynn and Amy Boyles for their persistence and vision. Also, to Betty Bolté and C.E. Irwin for catching my hiccups and mistakes and helping polish this story.

Finally, much love and appreciation to my family for never tiring of my zany, crazy antics. Thanks to you all, even our beloved tuxedo wearing resident guardian cat, Chali2Na.

# CHAPTER ONE

IT WAS LIKE the first time she'd laid eyes on him. The sun glistened off his back making him appear like a fabled demigod. His muscles rippled and caused her brain to short-circuit enough to hear a mysterious Bedouin song playing inside her mind, reeling her in with its rhythmic trance of lust. And it was lust. Pure unadulterated lust that made her breathe in deeply and then exhale with sheer appreciation of the man. Even knowing it was lust, Cassidy Spencer stood on the curb of 214 Loveless Lane cemented to the sidewalk watching the man she'd wanted for more years than not as he stripped the final lights from the high gabled roofline, no shirt required, even in the cold of January. Well, it wasn't that cold at sixty-two degrees on an unusually warm, sunny winter's day in Northern Alabama. But still, it was January. He ought to be shot for tempting her hormones up there half naked as he was.

Cassidy pulled herself together, remembered the packed bags sitting in her car parked in the driveway, and forged forward with her agenda fueling her every step. The sooner she got this over with, the sooner she would be on the road to a much needed getaway for one. This Christmas season had beaten her and left her bare. She needed to have a sit-down with herself concerning the state of affairs of her love life. Or lack of love life. There was no better way for that to happen than to get away from the mountain and her people to some place all alone. To think. To plan. To initiate a new year, a new life. A life clearly *without* Ben Murray and the ridiculous ways he clung to that his grandfather had drilled into him regarding the business of life. The elder Murray, God rest his soul, departed this earth over four years ago. There had been plenty of time since then for Ben to adjust his own thinking, to make changes, to be his own man. Clearly, if she was to have a life filled with love and a family of her own, she was the one who would have to change direction. Ben was never going to regard her as anything more than a business manager and friend.

As she reached the bottom of the ladder Ben was using, Dicker came flying around the corner of the house scaring the bejesus out of her with his top volume orders.

"Stop right there and bring yourself down off that ladder, Mr. Murray! You are *not* authorized to take my lights down!" Dicker stopped and slammed both hands onto his hips as he looked up to the top of the ladder. The sight of him made Cassidy smile. His fun-sized body appeared exaggeratedly toppled backwards while the port of his belly greeted the sky. He looked like a cartoon character.

Ben audibly sighed and looked over his shoulder down at the other man. "Dicker, we went through this last year, man. Give it up." He returned his attention to the task of removing lights, essentially ignoring Dicker.

Dicker sputtered as he stepped back a few yards to gain a better hollering angle. "The Homeowners' Association bylaws say. . ."

"I know what they say, Dicker. And this is not negotiable. The Skyline Fire Marshall overrides your rules."

"Dad blasted man! My lights are in impeccable condition. There is no need to examine them! That man only wants to shut me down for next year."

Cassidy watched Dicker as his face rapidly changed from pink to a red glow. He was mad and growing madder by the second. "Umm. Mr.

Dickerson?"

Dicker spun on her so fast the grass kicked out behind him. "Don't you start in on me, little missy. And the name's Dicker. Get with the program, will you?" He snarled and turned back to sky-high Ben. "You come down off that ladder this instant boy or I'll pull you off of there myself!"

"No can do, Dicker." Ben spoke calmly over his shoulder again and smiled. "I have one last strand to wind up and I'm done. If you've got an issue with this job you can take it up with the Fire Marshall. I'm only doing what he assigned me to do as a volunteer."

Ben wrapped the cord of lights he was working on, then added them to a hook on his belt. Simultaneously, as he started his descent to the earth, Dicker took off at a full bull run and kicked the extension ladder with all his might.

Cassidy watched in disbelief from another universe as the next ten-hour-long seconds played out. Realization hit Dicker the moment his foot left the metal rails of the ladder. It was as if that ladder, with Ben no more than three rungs from the top, was connected to a puppet string somewhere high in the sky, peeling both man and metal towards the ground in a slow motion scene of horror for all to witness. The air stuck in Cassidy's lungs and paralyzed her whole body long enough for her to see Ben turn his face to hers in shock and terror.

She took off at a run, to what she didn't know. Dicker visibly wilted as he prayed out loud to God for his sins and frailties. Ben wrestled to turn his body, grasped the forty-eight-foot extension ladder with his hands behind him readying for the inevitable landing. Someone from the street slammed on their brakes and started screaming. Cassidy turned and saw Jon Frazier's truck angled in the road so as to stop the ladder from hitting the concrete, hopefully placing Ben in the yard across the way. As Ben's fall accelerated, his legs dangled from the ladder downward into the air powered by gravity. Jon positioned himself as close as possible to Ben's destination so as to call on apparent emergency skills. Cassidy changed direction and took off running alongside the ladder, telling herself with every step, *He's going to be okay. We've got this. He's going to be okay. He's going to be okay.*

As if professionally choreographed, metal scraped and groaned as the ladder hit the roof of Jon's truck, levering Ben towards the ground. Nearing the hard dormant surface of the wheat colored grass, Ben reflexively reached out a hand, followed it with the other, and then slammed hard into the ground. He groaned. A collective sigh was heard from the others as the ladder popped back from releasing its occupant. Ben exhaled his relief as he rested on hands and knees. Jon took a step toward him to check for injuries but before he could reach his friend, who had barely leaned back on his haunches, the ladder came down a second time with all its might and slammed Ben in the head, forcing him to the ground with a loud thud. Cassidy screamed. Dicker grasped his heart and began stumbling around, shaking his head in denial of cause and effect. Jon hopped to it, lifted the ladder from Ben's head, and began checking for a pulse as he yelled "Call 911! NOW!"

DINGS AND BEEP-BEEP-BEEPS bounced off the cavernous walls of the emergency room. Cassidy positioned herself in full view of the double doors that divided her from where Ben's caregivers investigated his condition. Her fingers ached from digging into the hard molded chair, but she ignored her own discomfort, staying on point and watching as Jon filled Bear in on the details. While her mind wanted her to throw up, her body didn't remember how. She felt cold and disconnected. Jon, Ben, and Bear had been friends practically their whole lives. It served reason that Bear would be there. They were like brothers, the three of them.

Mama Paula, Bear's mother, who everyone around town counted as their own mother, pushed through double doors wearing her volunteer uniform and sat down next to Cassidy. She pulled Cassidy into her arms and cooed. "I hear you've had a rough day, sugar."

Cassidy let her head fall onto the elder woman's shoulder. "Has it only been one day?"

They sat there for who knows how long with Bear and Jon taking turns pacing and occasionally asking a question of the other. Each time someone came through the interior doors, they all stiffened, waiting for the staff member who appeared to call one of their names.

After a while, a doctor came through to ask for the family of one *Mr. Dickerson*.

Jon rolled his eyes.

Bear growled.

Mama Paula called Dicker an idiot.

Cassidy watched the room to see who, if anyone, came forward. Her heart sank at the lack of response. Even someone as curmudgeonly as Dicker deserved a loved one. Of course, they probably didn't deserve him, no one did. But still.

The doctor checked his clipboard and then called the name out a second time, louder as he scanned the room for any sign of movement.

A petite woman with hair the color of the sun at its highest point in the sky emerged quietly from around the corner of the waiting room. Her eyes held unwaveringly on the doctor with the clipboard as she slowly moved toward him. A young man followed closely behind her, talking too loudly on a cell phone, saying something about an account that he couldn't afford to lose and that he had no choice in the matter of being at the hospital. When he recognized everyone in the smaller waiting area was watching him closely, he reluctantly added, "It's my father." He held everyone's rapt attention then. Before closing the call, he added tightly, "I'll be in touch," and slipped the phone into his trouser pocket.

Curiosity got the best of Cassidy's attention. She stretched her ears in the direction of the new arrivals on the scene. She leaned in and whispered to Mama Paula. "I didn't think Dicker had a family. Did you?"

"Nope." Mama Paula drew that one syllable word out and then up high like a whistle at the end. She sat tall and straight and crossed her arms tight across her chest. One short leg went quickly over the other and her foot began bouncing to the beat of I've-got-to-hear-*THIS*-story! She didn't bother leaning forward. She simply waited. Everybody knew she possessed incredible bionic-mama-hearing.

Cassidy leaned in, bracing herself on her knees to hear every word.

Bear and Jon stood at a safe distance, but they too were zeroed in on the conversation taking place.

The younger man reached out a hand to greet

the attending doctor. "I'm Mr. Dickerson's son." He placed a hand on the woman's shoulder and gently urged her forward. "This is my mother, Mrs. Dickerson."

The doctor nodded his greeting. "Perhaps you could help settle Mr. Dickerson so we can take some tests. He's a little," the doctor reached up and smoothed an invisible mustache, "shall we say, high-strung?"

This elicited a round of nodding heads and various mumblings from everyone looking on.

Concern washed over the woman's features. "Is he going to be okay, doctor?"

"Actually, I think he's healthy as a newborn babe. But, since he's insisting he had a heart attack, I have to run a few tests. It's mainly for our peace of mind." He winked at her and smiled." You do understand, right?"

Mrs. Dickerson's shoulders relaxed as she agreed. "I understand he's probably acting a fool, as usual." She moved to make eye contact with lead-heckler-Mama Paula and sighed.

Mama Paula shook her head and turned away.

Dicker's son piped up, taking charge. "Well then, let's get this over with. Lead the way and we'll make him cooperate."

As Dicker's family wound their way to the great inside, the double doors once again swung open, releasing a man from its clutches whose hair had long ago disappeared save for the reach-out-and-touch-someone eyebrows the color of smoke. His shoulders slumped, from years of chart reading no doubt. A foggy haze bathed his eyes in muck that surely he could not see past. Words croaked from his mouth undiscernible. He cleared his throat, covered his mouth with the boney back side of his hand, coughed, and offered a do over with more gusto. "I've got a Mr. Murray in here. Says he has no family." He drew in another fortifying breath. "Anyone want to claim him?"

Before Cassidy could shout out "Yes!" Ben swaggered through the doors, stopped at the doctor's side, snatched the pen out of the doctor's hand, and scratched what could only be guessed as his signature. Then he did something so alarming, Cassidy fell back into her seat and gasped.

The man actually had the audacity to find her eyes, lift his own lips into a sultry, sexy, how-you-doin' grin. And then he winked at her. Ben. He winked at her, Cassidy Spencer. Ben Murray, the object of the Cassidy Spencer Hormone Society of One, bold facedly, in front of the sun and stars, the moon and the entire universe, winked at her, Cassidy Spencer. *What. The. Hell.* And from there he sauntered to the doors that led outside, threw a hand into the sky and waved his final farewell. He was off and out. Over and done. On his own. Healthy as a newborn babe but clearly out of his frickin' mind.

"Somebody better go watch after that boy. I'm not sure he was officially released." Mama Paula shooed at the men to catch up to Ben. "Y'all go! Cassidy and I will figure out this end. But keep those phones handy. I'll bet we've got us some loose ends to tie up."

And she was off and running, directing and barking like she herself was in charge. Well, who was kidding whom? Mama Paula was always in charge no matter the title or location.

# CHAPTER TWO

CASSIDY WAS MOMENTARILY glued to her seat trying to take it all in and make sense of Ben's actions. Why would he wink at her? Why would he look at her like that, undressing her and licking her from one end of her body to the other all in point zero zero zero three seconds? And lord have mercy on her sinful, lustful soul, where on God's green pastures did he find that swagger he was sporting? It had her steaming up from the inside out and made her want more of him.

From there a bit of craziness ensued, what with doctors demanding, nurses fussing, and Mama Paula going Mama-Drama on them all. Cassidy couldn't take it anymore. She slipped out to her car, glared at her luggage, made a phone call to cancel her reservations, and then headed to the office. Surely that's where he would go. It's always where he went. Ben the business man. All business. No play. Every hour, every day.

Surprisingly when she arrived at The River Rat Boat Rentals and Cottages office, the doors were locked and showed no sign of Ben. She let herself in, adjusted the thermostat, fluttered around, piddling with this and that to pass the time. She gathered the mail, shredded the junk mail, and made a change to a reservation that came in over the phone.

Finally, she decided to stay where she was to wait it out, let Jon and Bear handle Ben. They were more family to him anyway. Surely, Mama Paula would call when there was news. Sitting down at her desk, she powered up her computer and started playing with her toys. Finance sheets, stocks and bonds, forecasts and whatnot filled the afternoon hours. As the sun began its final slip past the tree line, Cassidy remembered she'd dropped Ben's phone in her bag at the hospital. She retrieved it, looked to see if there were any messages but couldn't maneuver past the home screen without a password. She placed it inside the desk for when Ben came back to the office. Then for the billionth time that afternoon, she checked her own phone. Worry settled in.

No calls.
No texts.
No emails.

BEN STOOD IN his bedroom trying to wrap his head around his personal identity crisis. Clearly he'd experienced an accident, but the only thing he could remember was wrapping wires and pondering what it would it be like to allow Cassidy into his life on a more intimate level. Why he couldn't do such a thing was beyond him. She looked good enough to eat. It simply didn't make any sense at all to not let her in.

He shook his head at himself. But then, what did he know? Not a lot. Here he stood in a completely unfamiliar place trying to figure out if he should be alone or attached.

Merely a half-hour ago Bear and Jon found him sauntering down a street near the hospital. Of course, he had no idea where he was going so he'd gladly accepted the ride they offered to his house. And while this location didn't match the address on his driver's license, he went with it, assuming they knew better than he did given the circumstances. They were nice enough guys, he decided, as they chatted along the way. They seemed to know each other very well, tried enveloping him with their talk too, leaving Ben to conclude that they must be good friends, the three of them. Ben hadn't offered any input to their conversation. No, he simply enjoyed the ride and took in the details they offered. He'd been careful to listen and learn what was what, especially since the last thing the ER doctor said to him was that his accident had sparked some sort of temporary memory loss. That worked for Ben since he'd been forced to check his wallet for an ID to learn what his own name was. Thankfully, he remembered enough about the practical things of life to know that he carried a wallet. After that, the doctor had gone all technical on Ben with his terminology and risks and all. That was when Ben decided he'd had enough of his hospital visit. He escaped the first chance he got, wearing a scrub shirt he'd found on his way out of the ER interior.

So here he was now, minus Jon and Bear. They'd had someplace to go once they were convinced by a lot of nodding on Ben's part that he could settle himself into his own cabin without their help. Though, it was really half of a cabin, the backside of the offices of The River Rat Boat Rentals and Cottages. Thankfully, it offered a private entrance so he could avoid whoever's car that was parked at the office. Time to put his mind into gear, to try puzzling out who he really was, beyond the photo and the specs of the person on his license.

The room's windows were framed by a dark stained wood worn with years of opening and closing. A small bureau sat against one wall, its mirror large and proud. There wasn't a thing sitting on top, the drawers neatly pushed in all the way. A rug lay across what looked to be a very old and beautifully maintained hardwood floor. Ben ran a hand through his hair where he was reminded of the knot on his head. Right. A concussion. Pretty big bump on the noggin, too. He let out a sigh as he turned to quietly open the closet door to take stock of his wardrobe and search for clues. A hook hung over the inside of the door, empty but clearly used if the semicircle scraping of wood underneath it was an indicator. It was probably where he hung the tool belt Jon had handed him on his way in from the truck. He retrieved the belt from beside the entry door where he'd placed it and looped it over the closet door's hook. Sure enough, the worn places on the wood matched where the belt's hardware met the leather that held his various hand tools.

Inside the closet a long cord hung from the ceiling to engage the overhead light when pulled. The guts of the inside were pretty sparse. A black suit hung toward the back with a silk tie rolled up and stored in the breast pocket, a dress belt slipped over the hook of the hanger. Funerals, weddings, and such, he figured. The coat pocket held a jewelry box with a tie clasp inside. Between him and the suit hung two white shirts, a couple of black and red plaid flannel shirts, and a smattering of dark colored jeans. A worn-to-softness pair of khaki canvas pants were tucked to the right side, possibly forgotten about. Neatly on the floor sat a shiny pair of black dress shoes and a well-used pair of running shoes with an empty space in between, probably for the work boots he was currently wearing.

What interested Ben most was what hung in the very center of the closet, wrapped in a clear plastic bag, likely a dry cleaning bag, all neat and tidy. A kilt. Huh. What the devil did a man need a kilt for? He retrieved the package from the clothes rod, which on closer examination held more than one hanger, and laid it out on the bed for a closer look. Laying in front of him were three kilts, not one. Each one was made of a red and black plaid with a shiny silver thread woven through the fabric. All three were in impeccable condition, soft and beautiful in craftsmanship. Curious.

Ben went back to the bureau to check its contents. Upon opening the top drawer, he found socks and underwear, all black and neatly organized. The next drawer held t-shirts that were folded and stacked with the skill of a very good launderer or someone who was obsessed with order. At least a dozen shirts in all. He ran a hand across the front stack, flipping them like pages of a book. All were in excellent condition. *Good Lord, he was a neat freak.*

He opened the bottom drawer last. Inside was a bright yellow athletic t-shirt, two pairs of running shorts, a pair of pants with a stripe the same yellow as the t-shirt down the side seam, and two pairs of board shorts. Laying on top of it all was a whistle on a rope. Interesting. But he'd saved the best for last, the small drawers on the top of the piece of furniture that were likely meant for jewelry or keepsakes of some type. He opened the one on the right to find a velvet box. Inside was a diamond ring and matching band. The band was engraved with an infinity symbol. Underneath the inner velvet was another band, this one larger, obviously for a man. Unlike the other, it was not engraved. Was he getting married? Ben scanned his mind but couldn't recall a woman in his life except for the thoughts of Cassidy before the accident. He reflected on seeing her at the hospital. He wouldn't mind having her in his life. She was a looker!

He replaced the rings into their nest and closed them away. In the drawer to the left was a set of keys, each labeled and numbered, RRC 1 through RRC 7, and another one simply labeled RRCO. An engraved metal tag stated the keyring's purpose, *RRC Spare.* So he really was the man who ran these cabins on the river. Again, he replaced the contents of the drawer. Then he removed the wallet from his back pocket and laid its contents on top of the bureau to examine. A driver's license that said he lived on Skyline Mountain Road. Good man. He was an organ donor. An insurance card for an old truck, liability only. Cheapskate. A Visa debit card for Riverland National Bank. A piece of paper with a name and number scrawled across it and today's date. The name was Catherine. A relative maybe? The number was local. Underneath the name and number were the words, return by six. Weird. He didn't know what to make of that piece of information. There were also a few twenty-dollar bills, an old picture of a school-aged girl with Cassidy Spencer printed on the back in very neat handwriting (though, the e's were backward), and a receipt from Henry's Bar B and Cue for a pulled pork sandwich and a beer. That was it. That was the entire contents of his wallet.

Ben scrubbed a hand across his face, his growth of stubble scratched his palm, versed the air with its sound. He looked around the room before proceeding ahead through the only other visible door. The bathroom. Inside the shower was an inexpensive bottle of shampoo and a bar of soap half used. The medicine cabinet was empty save for a tube of toothpaste, a toothbrush, and a stick of deodorant. A towel hung on the towel rod, fresh and clean. A spare was folded neatly and laid on the tank of the toilet. Ben closed the door to check if there was anything on the back side. Nope. Not even a hook.

Ben didn't know what to make of his life. He leaned over the sink, bracing his arms on the counter to stare into eyes he didn't recognize. They weren't brown. They weren't green. They were eyes the color of in-between, whatever that was. His hair was straight and dark, barely long enough to hang in his eyes and pester him. Peering into the mirror, he spoke out loud, questioning his identity to himself. "Who?" Confusion quickly followed like before, at the hospital, when he had answered questions for the doctor. He'd sounded funny, even to himself. Then *and* now, though the doctor paid no mind to it at all.

Ben cleared his throat and gave it another try. "Who urr. . ." He stopped, quirked an eye at his reflection in response to the "r" sound that rolled off his lips. He straightened himself and, placing his hands on his hips, coughed in preparation for yet another attempt, hoping to get a handle on his deep baritone voice. He shook his head, signaling to himself that he was ready, and pushed his words out into the empty air. "Who arr yeh, Benjamin Murree?"

Ben's mouth dropped open, his jaw hung wide. His mind raced in thought of what he was seeing and hearing. In his own head he sounded like everyone else he'd heard that day, speaking perfectly good and normal English.

Deciding to give it another go, Ben thought of something to say and first tested it inside his mind. *My name is Benjamin Murray.* He cleared his throat, hoping, and gave his mouth another shot to say exactly what he'd thought. Oddly, what came out of his mouth was not at all what he'd imagined.

"They ca' me Benjamin Murree."

Ben's eyes grew big as the details combined to form a conclusive idea in his mind. The r's convinced him with their deep embellishment of his name. Mix that together with the kilts, the cheap insurance, and, for all that's holy, comprehension hit him upside his head like the proverbial iron skillet. He threw both hands high in the air in recognition of who he was and pumped his arms in quiet celebration. "A'm a *Scot!*"

Frustration melted away into fascination as he began pacing the small spaces of his home. He tried to wrap his mind around all of it. The Scottish brogue combined with his wallet contents and the surroundings of his home made for a very interesting individual. At some point he simply started talking out loud to himself, trying on his new persona and acquainting himself with *Ben the Scot.* When he'd all but worn a new rut into the wood floors, he stopped pacing. "Wha th' devil am ah t' do *now?*"

He fell onto the bed, crossed his legs at the ankles, and raised his arms to prop his head up in thought. If he was a Scot, and he owned land, then he was a *rich* Scot! Never mind the odd phone number with the name Catherine and its return date and time. He owned kilts and land, and he was a neat freak and a cheapskate, which was probably how he'd gained his wealth. Or he was simply cheap, and well, that was okay with a Scot, too.

Now that he had a jump-start on his identity, Ben decided it was time to get out and about town where he could learn from the locals more of who he really was. So he freshened up and prepared for an adventure in self-discovery. Then it occurred to him, if he was a Scot with a kilt, maybe there was a dagger or a sword somewhere, too. And off he went to see what he could find.

CASSIDY COULD NOT believe the sight displayed for all the world to see right there in front of her very own eyeballs. Straight ahead, far in the back hall of Henry's, was a loud and randy Scotsman. A likely loud, and randy, and *very drunk* Scotsman. Except she knew this man. He was no Scotsman. He was her first love, her one and only true love from all the way back to elementary school. He was one very confused Benjamin Thomas Murray. Cassidy could not believe the spectacle he was providing for the locals.

She turned her head as Henry came around the bar. He slapped a towel over his shoulder and nodded in her direction. He motioned for her to join him at the bar's end nearest to the door. Laughter bellowed from the far reaches of the pool room.

Cassidy shuddered and gave thanks for the place not being any more crowded than it was.

"I'm so glad you're here, Cassidy. I knew you'd come right away." Henry wiped his forehead with the back of his beefy hand. "That boy ain't right, I tell you. He's been drinking and carousing since he stepped into the place late this afternoon." He shook his head, worry crossing his features. "I left messages all around town for Jon and Bear but they haven't returned my calls."

"Henry, what on earth has he done?" She jumped at the sound of a loud "whack" coming from Ben's general direction. Ben used a pool stick to fence against someone she didn't know. "Start at the top and tell me everything." She scooted up onto a bar stool.

"Child, he came in here proud as you please, sporting that kilt, first of all. Started barking orders like he owned the place himself. Then that boy marched right up behind *my* bar, scanned the contents of *my* wall and pulled *my only* bottle of The Glenlivet down and took a swig *straight from the bottle*. I swancy, Cass! That boy ain't got a lick of sense right now. He's been taking pulls off that bottle going on two hours. He's lost his ever loving mind, he has." Henry huffed loudly, shook his fist in the air, and inhaled another for round two. "Then! *Then*, I tell you! He proceeded to march back to *my* pool room calling players as he went. *In brogue*, no less! That young man?" Henry pointed at Ben's form again for double emphasis, his eyes bulging beyond their sockets. "That man thinks he's a damn *Scot*! I want him out of here, Cass. *Out*!"

Right on cue to enhance and end Henry's tirade, a pool stick flew through the doorway between the dining room and the pool room, slamming against a chair before rattling to the floor. A man sitting at the piano stopped playing to take stock of the situation. He raised an eyebrow at Henry in question.

Cassidy reached across the bar and patted the elder's hand for assurance. "Thank you for calling me, Henry. Don't you worry. I'll get him out of your hair. Fast!"

"You don't understand, sugar. He's not only drinking and living it up himself, but he's buying rounds for everyone in the house! If I didn't know that was Ben Murray I'd say it was normal. But that's not normal for Ben. You and I *both* know it!"

Another round of laughter broke out, coughing up a man from the bowels of the back room. Ben staggered toward Cassidy sporting a kilt, his work boots, and a tee shirt that clung to every muscle the man owned above his waistline.

Cassidy groaned inside. This was not going to be good. Her gut squeezed. She felt a bit of a flutter of warning inside her stomach. Or was that lust? She couldn't tell which with him looking at her like

24

his next meal, and for the second time that day! Ben continued to swagger her way, his face split wide into a grin. He reached up with one hand to rub the hard rippled planes of his middle. If she didn't know better she would've sworn she heard him growl. Eight feet away from her, someone scooted their chair back, bumping into him walking past. Ben lost his already shaky balance, teetered toward another table, then hit it hard enough that the newly filled pitcher of beer toppled over and spilled directly into a man's lap. The man didn't look one bit happy about it.

Ben grappled with the empty pitcher, offering his apologies to the man. He lifted the pitcher high into the air and boldly stated, "Another round for mah pal!" He stood, wobbled, and dusted himself off. "An' put it oan mah tab, jimmy."

Cassidy gave him a hard stare as she placed her hands on her hips. As she began to speak, Ben caught the attention of onlookers. "She's a bonny lass, isn' she mates?" Ben walked up to her without a speck of remorse, placed a hand around her bottom, and pulled her hard against his body.

Cassidy slapped both hands on his chest and shoved hard.

Ben didn't budge.

"You are out of control, Benjamin Murray. Let me go right this instant!" She pushed at him, trying to get away.

People around began laughing and cheering him on. Henry tried to step in, but Ben pushed him away to slip around Cassidy's neck to whisper something in her ear. She wasn't certain what he said, but it sounded something remotely like a woman named Wilma Makemah, her dreams and the night, or some such. Geesh! What did she know about brogue? It made as much sense as pig Latin to her.

Cassidy was ready to pull out the stops and kick the man in his jewels, but before she could act a familiar voice shouted out Ben's name across the room. Everyone went silent. Bear Grecco marched over to Ben, picked him up by the scruff of his shirt, and set him away from Cassidy. "You owe the lady an apology." He waited for Ben to comply.

Aggravation bounced off of Ben. "Who are yeh tae tell me what tae dae?" He stood taller, ready to fight.

"Oh shush, the both of you!" Cassidy wanted to move Ben out of the public eye lickety-split so they could figure out what the heck was going on. "Henry, send his tab to me at the office. I'll settle up with you." She aimed her attention at Bear. "Let's move it! Get him to my car, will you?"

The crowd jeered their offense. "But you said beer on the house for the rest of the night," someone yelled out.

Cassidy couldn't find the heckler, but she

addressed the entire room of customers. "Sorry, y'all. This man has suffered a severe trauma to the head. He can't pay for your drinks for the rest of the night. You're all cut off as of right now."

Ben stumbled around Bear. With a drunken slur almost as heavy as his accent, he said, "Ah d'no' lik' yer wit, lassie."

"Yeah? Well I don't like anything about *you* right at this moment, Ben." She slapped Henry on the shoulder. "I'll take care of that bill as soon as you send it to me and I can get to the bank. In the morning is fine with me. Good enough?"

She waited for him to approve. Henry's head bobbed in agreement. Cassidy slipped an arm around Ben's elbow as Bear pulled his other arm toward the exit. Together the three of them got the hell out of there as fast as Bear could drag them to safety.

The cold front that rolled in earlier that day hit them full force as soon as they exited the building. Bear's phone rang. It was Jon. Bear kept moving them towards their destination. Cassidy couldn't tell what they were discussing on the phone, but she did hear the words "Damn Scot!" loud and clear. Bear crammed Ben into his beater truck before getting behind the wheel himself.

"I'll meet you at the office, Cass. Jon'll be there, too. We've got to figure this out before it gets any worse." With that, he was off.

Cassidy rushed to her own car and pulled up right behind them, anxious to put things in order

.

# CHAPTER THREE

CASSIDY SAT NEXT to Ben's side on a collapsible camping stool in the storeroom that separated the offices from his private side of the cabin. The room was equipped with an exit door for loading and unloading supplies, a small kitchenette, in addition to the door leading to Ben's personal rooms, the latter of which was dead bolted from the opposite side for his personal privacy. The room they sat in also housed a cot in case it was ever needed for first aid. Clearly there was never a time more needed than now. Though this particular exploration (one Ben Murray, drunk, concussed, and apparently with loss of his memory) was not one she'd ever dreamed she'd need to rescue and administer aid to. She'd spent the past half hour or more talking Ben down from spinning walls, trying to convince him to sleep off the drunken stupor he had acquired. Ben wasn't playing well with her efforts. He kept rambling on and on about ideas he had that seemed to have little to no connection with each other. At one point she wondered if he wasn't simply enamored with his newly acquired accent. At the moment he was voicing new opinions of women, opinions Cassidy knew for certain he did *not* hold in his real heart and soul.

"You're a bonny lass, Cassidy. Ah like th' way yer eyes shimmer like th' color o' th' sea rippling back and forth from blue to green at night's fall." His face relaxed into a sleepy smile. "You're a bonnie lass, you are!" He extended a hand up to touch her face.

Cassidy felt compromised within herself. She knew full well Ben Murray did *not* have feelings or admirations for her, Cassidy Spencer. He made that clear a very long time ago. To this day it made her sad that he didn't want her.

But he touched her with softness as he whispered once again. "Mak' mah dreams come true t' night, Cassi." His hand slipped silkily down her neck, arm, past her elbow, and across her hand. His touch stilled on hers, long enough for Cassidy to wonder if he'd finally found sleep. Then he moved her hand with his own, slipped it across his stomach, reaching down to place her hand around himself, letting her feel where his thoughts had landed. On her. On them. Together.

Cassidy jumped and fell over her chair backwards trying to get away from him. Lordy but he was mighty big and aroused! In the commotion, she heard Mama Paula ask from the office if everything was alright. Alright? *Alright? Are you kidding me? There was absolutely nothing about this day or night that was all right!* She scooped herself up and squeaked out a response, trying her best not to cause further alarm on the other side of the door. When she set the chair back upright on its three legs, she prepared to give Ben a piece of her mind, whispered of course, only to find him with a smile on his face, a hand proudly upon his privates, a serene snore escaping past his lips.

"BOYS, I DON'T have the time or the know-how to take this on." Mama Paula did not appear happy to have been pulled away from her monthly book club. Not so much because of the book but because book club was the heartbeat of what's what in Riverland. And tonight she was supposed to find out who was coming home to stay. Gran Raine had promised to make the announcement over cake and coffee and Mama Paula missed it all, everything past the initial greetings of the night. And for what? For these boys to dump on her? "He named the two of you, one after the other, as his Power of Attorney, not me."

"I understand that, Mama Paula. But I can't do this. I'm barely able to keep up with my own business right now." Jon aimed his head in the direction of where Cassidy was trying to settle Ben close by so she could keep an eye on him for the night. "Besides, he made those choices more than ten years ago. He has a lot more at stake nowadays than what he had then. I'm not even sure I'd know where to start."

Mama Paula directed her attention straight at her own son, commanding without speaking a word.

"I can't do it either." Bear crossed his arms over the wall of his big bad self. "I leave for Italy in two days to teach a class at the University for six weeks. You know that, Mama. And no, I'm not canceling. It's already been rescheduled twice in the past eight months. Besides," he said as he pushed back in his chair letting it rock perilously on two feet, "Julia's never been overseas. She's meeting me there after my class for a spring break vacation." He grinned suggestively and wiggled his eyebrows. "I won't be stateside for ten weeks."

Mama Paula slapped her hand at the air towards Bear and shook her head, completely missing the fact that her boy was leaning back in his chair contrary to all that she'd taught him his whole life long. "Boys, I know this is not a good time."

She threw her hands up into the air. "Heck! It's never a good time for an emergency!" She fell back into her chair. "I can't do this because, frankly, I'm not qualified. I don't know a thing about his business *or* his holdings. I'd do more harm than good for that boy and you both know it." She stood and shoved her hands into her trouser pockets, clearly deliberating what to do. A loud sound came from behind the door.

"You alright in there, Cassidy?" Mama Paula spoke to the door.

"I'm fine, thanks," came the weak response.

Mama Paula frowned in question to Cassidy's response before returning her attention back to the business at hand. "Well, I don't know what to do exactly, but like his lawyer said on the phone, if you don't take it on, Jon, then it falls to Bear. And, Bear, if you don't take it on, then you have to find someone who is capable of the task of overseeing all of his affairs. You can't slide this onto someone else's plate haphazardly. You're going to have to find someone who knows his business or is capable of getting up to speed *fast*. Someone trustworthy and honest or you two will have to be up in the big middle of it all, regardless of your own times and needs. That's what you agreed to when he asked you to cover his back."

A door swung open quietly. Cassidy eased into the office. "He's out," she said in response to the questioning eyes. "He's in a dead sleep, happy in his own private dream world."

"Well, his private world just got a bit bigger," Mama Paula complained. "And one of you will have to step up to the plate." She gave them all a hard looksy. "Which one of you can stand up to him and keep his affairs best in order, including those ridiculous miserly standards his grandfather instilled in him?" Her hands were on her hips now, in full drama mode, eyeing each one of them in turn.

Jon stood and invited Cassidy to take her desk chair back. She felt out of place in the midst of this emergency. Ben had never let her closer than arm's length even though they'd known each other longer than they had not. No, he wouldn't approve even now, she was certain of it. But then he wouldn't approve of Mama Paula being mixed up in this mess, either. It had nothing to do with their skills or lack of them but everything to do with their gender. Ben Murray, contrary to his earlier behavior, was not a fan of women in charge or meddling in his personal business. With one exception. Cassidy was his business manager because there simply was no one better at it than her. But then, his grandfather was who hired her, not Ben. She knew Ben's business of the rentals and cottages inside and out, backwards and forwards. The only thing about it she didn't know was how to repair a boat. But that was beside the point.

"I was telling the boys that they're either going to have to muster up and take this responsibility to heart or find someone they can trust to do the job right. What do you think, Cassidy? Do you know anyone who Ben would trust his affairs to other than us?"

As the last words came out of Mama Paula's mouth, Jon and Bear peered at each other. A kind of silent language passed between them and left each of them nodding their understanding before turning to look at Cassidy in unison.

Cassidy's stomach ached at the directive they aimed at her. She felt the floor drop out from underneath her. Darkness shrouded the room around her. Suddenly, the air thinned. Realization slammed into her mind like a tank. They were looking to her as Ben's savior. They were asking her to take this on and run with it. They were making her the bad guy to keep Ben safe. Ben would forever hate her afterwards. If there was to be an afterwards. If he ever regained his memory. Bile bit at the back of her throat. She couldn't breathe. Both of the men in front of her beamed as they recognized her awareness.

Mama Paula jumped out of her chair and squealed. "I have the perfect solution y'all! Let's have Cassidy handle his affairs!"

Cassidy couldn't make her words form or

sound them out for anyone to hear. All she could do was tell her head to move, to negate their requests, to turn from side to side.

Mama Paula clapped her hands together in joy.

Horror enveloped Cassidy, clenching her heart in its grip.

Bear let his chair fall back to the floor. "This is perfect, Cass! You already know all of the details concerning the business. Hell, you run the whole thing anyway. Surely you know his personal finances and such, right? It's a piece of cake for you!"

Jon stood, and then stretched his shoulders, showing his relief to have this little dilemma solved.

Mama Paula piped up. "And Cassidy! Sugar pie, this is perfect because you can use those fancy investment skills of yours to make everything even better for Ben. He'll be so proud when he comes back around! You'll see."

"What investment skills?" Worry covered Bear's features. "You play the stocks, Cassidy?"

"It's more than playing the stocks, son. She's a money genius! It's like her thing. Her hobby. She can turn air into gold, she can!"

Jon shook his head and let out a low whistle of concern. "Well, it's going to *take* a genius to sidestep Ben's irrational fear of spending money." He set out pacing the length of the room, jingling keys in his pocket nervously. "Of course, I don't have to tell you that, Cass."

Cassidy sat, her eyes grew wild as fear beat at her insides.

Jon paced back towards Mama Paula. "What about that other little detail?"

"Oh yes, right, son. Doc says we can't tell him anything, either. He'll be better off remembering things on his own, so mum's the word, alrighty?" She made a motion to zip her lips for everyone to agree with her.

"No." Cassidy stood and placed both hands flat on her desk, commanding everyone's attention. "No!" Finally, she could speak, thank the Lord above. "You all can *not* ask me to do this. You know what he thinks about women in charge. I can't, y'all. I can't do this. It's not right. Ben would never forgive me for this." Her eyes searched her spectators for agreement or assurance or understanding. Compassion, at the very least. But all she saw staring back at her was a round of smiles.

Bear gave her a two thumbs up. "You've got this, Cass!"

Jon laughed as he agreed with Bear.

Mama Paula all but did a little dance of cheer for her, front and center.

Cassidy lifted her waste paper basket and proceeded to throw up.

THE FOLLOWING MORNING, after waking up in the office's foldout chair, Cassidy quickly did her business before peeking in on Ben in the storeroom. He was still sprawled out on the cot, sawing logs. His kilt lay askew, revealing his strong legs. His t-shirt bunched up in the middle, a hand slipped under it as if he'd been rubbing his belly. Contrary to his brawny body, in sleep, Ben Murray looked like an angel. His lips were pink and soft, his hair fell loosely over his cheeks. Peace washed across his face. She gave herself time to admire his serenity. In sleep he was heavenly and beautiful. In the light of day? Handsome and in control, yes. But tranquil? She couldn't remember a day when Ben wasn't stressed or behaving a bit uptight. He was always in a hurry to move on to the next job.

Well, that wasn't quite true. She could remember when they were very young he'd been laid back and easygoing. But then he'd grown up, filled with unreasonable expectations from his grandfather. He responded by placing a lead barrier between himself and everyone else in the entire world. No one was allowed in. He didn't allow his true self out, either. He was an island of a man living in isolation in the midst of a nest of people who loved and adored him. But it didn't matter. That's how he'd set his stage and he was guarding it like a sentinel.

Cassidy eased into the room. She carefully

opened the blinds of the small eastern window. Light flooded in, garnering a protest. Cassidy moved into his field of view, hoping for the old Ben to greet her. "Good morning."

Ben peeked at her through his fingers to keep the light at bay. "Please speak softer, lass."

Cassidy snickered. "I'm sure you feel awful, but it's time to face the day. There's work to be done, Benjamin Murray."

Ben groaned out loud as he turned his back to her.

She laughed quietly. "You can ignore me all you want, but the pipes in Cottage No. 3 need to be rewrapped before the bad weather hits at the end of the week. The Murdocks over on Mason Road called this morning, asking when you'd be by to take down their lights. You promised them they were on the schedule right after Dicker. You finished with Dicker yesterday, if you'll recall."

Ben rolled over to face Cassidy. He lifted himself slowly to a sitting position and groaned. "I'll get tae them as soon as somebo'y makes th' hammerin' in mah haed stop a'poundin'." He held his head gingerly, between his knees, breathing in deep and exhaling slowly. "But ah dae nae recall anyone by th' name o' Murdock."

"Yes, well you probably dae nae recall," she said mockingly, "that you don't drink alcohol either." She stared at him hard. "Ever."

Ben didn't look up. He simply moaned in her direction.

She offered a hand. "Come on, big boy. You go to your room and get cleaned up. I'll find you something for the pain along with some food to give you energy for the morning."

# CHAPTER FOUR

BEN FOUND CASSIDY true to her word. Upon returning to the office after a shower, she'd poured a beastly concoction down his throat, then fed and medicated him. For the most part, he felt better. It didn't hurt that she watched him throughout the meal with concern on her face. He liked her face. Come to think of it, he liked all of her other parts, too. Especially the parts that swayed when she walked away from him, tempting him to reach out and pull her back against him. He couldn't figure out why it was that she always broke free from his grasp, though. Especially since he recalled she'd been fond of him since grade school, loved him even, if he remembered correctly. But she sure was behaving strangely since he left the hospital yesterday, running away from him when he stepped too close. Twice now she'd run scared from his affections. He decided he would be better equipped to tussle with her later, after the day's work was done and he felt more renewed.

But the day had not gone so smoothly, what with the Murdock girls following him around. They tried to sneak a peek underneath his kilt, saying strange things before giggling behind their hands like a couple of pests. Mr. Murdock would do well to lock them in the cooler if he knew what was best for them. On his way back to the office, his truck coughed, sputtered, and then died on the side of the road. He saw no choice but to leave it behind and put one foot in front of the other.

As he walked, Ben considered a few details that pushed at his mind. He understood he was void of his identity, but why did he know how to drive a truck? How was it he hid the knowledge of plumbing inside his mind, but not the details of his family and upbringing, his friends? Where was the reasoning behind what he remembered and what he did not? And another thing, why was Cassie acting like he had the plague every time he went to touch her? As he'd left breakfast that morning, he'd reached over to kiss her cheek. She'd once again taken off running for a task "she'd forgotten."

He set the thoughts aside, focusing on the road and countryside around him. Did he grow up here? Nothing, not the cows on the hills or the river that ran alongside the road, incited any meaning whatsoever in his brain cells. The only solid memory he retained was the sense of affection from Cassie, but then that wasn't really a solid memory if her current actions were any indication. He *did* recognize a sign up ahead that hung dangerously sideways as if its days were numbered, though. But then it might be because he could read the sign, not actually remember the place. The sign read *Knights Garage*. Cars upon rows of cars lined the entrance underneath its faded colors. Surely, someone could help him repair his truck, get him back on the road.

Ben marched up the metal strewn drive and then through the office doors. He slapped a hand down on the counter good naturedly. "G'aftarenoon, Jimmy!"

The man, in a blue work shirt with the name "Charlie" embroidered in red, grunted without looking up at Ben from behind the counter.

"Mah truck seems t' ha' broken down an' needs a bit o' repair." He leaned over the counter to capture the man's attention. "Kin y' help me ou', mah frien'?" Ben let a smile lace his words, hoping to charm the man's attention.

"*Help* is it?" Charlie Knight stood at his full height, a hair above five and a half feet tall. He wrapped his arms around his midsection and crossed them. A voice on the radio behind him announced the time and launched a new song into play before Charlie spoke again. "The name's

Charlie. Charlie Knight. Not Jimmy, as you well know. Are you asking *me* for a bit of help with that rat-trap of a truck of yours, Benjamin Murray?"

"Aye, Ah believe A'am." Ben's optimism shone as bright as the sun on a warm summer's day in July.

Charlie turned his back to Ben to rumble around in something out of Ben's sight. Then he changed direction and charged himself around the corner of the counter, dressed in fury and wielding a Billy club in his fist.

Ben took off running, alarm fueling each step he took. Charlie came after him as fast as his body would propel him forward, yelling ugly words about payments denied and work not meeting standards. Ben picked up speed. Halfway down the entrance driveway, a dog caught up to him, barking and nipping at his skirt tails, trying to secure a piece of the kilt firmly into his mouth. Ben stopped and wrestled with the dog, all the while keeping an eye on Charlie Knight gaining on him. It wouldn't do to be unwrapped by a dog and beaten by a crazy mechanic after abandoning his truck on the side of the road, and all in the matter of a few morning hours. Where was his gentle Cassidy to take charge of the situation?

With only seconds to spare, Ben ripped the kilt away from the dog's mouth and took off at a full run. He heard a scuffle behind him. The dog yelped before Charlie let out a line of expletives only a convict would shout. Ben dared to look back around to see the man sprawled across the top of his guard dog in the dirt, with Charlie shaking his weapon in the wind at Ben.

With a chunk of fabric out of his hide, Ben continued to run until he reached the town limits. He checked to see if his phone would make a call. Before he could dial, Cassidy pulled up alongside of him.

"Get in!"

Never before had he been so glad to see someone, anyone, especially his girl with eyes full of kindness.

"You look like hell." Cassidy didn't give him time to buckle up before pulling away from the curb.

"Ah was attacked by a dug."

Cassidy quirked an eyebrow in question. "What's a 'dug'?"

Ben secured his seatbelt then dropped his head back on the headrest and sighed. He rubbed a hand over his heart in attempt to make it slow down. "'Twas th' beast wi' Charlie Knight."

Cassidy slammed on the brakes without warning. The sudden stop pitched Ben forward, painfully engaging his seat belt into action, binding him tightly to the seat.

"Bugger, Lass! Wha''re ye tryin' t' d' t' me,

murder?" Ben's eyes jutted out at her.

Cassidy shot her big eyes right back at him. "Tell me," she ground out, "you did *not* go to Knight's Garage for help with your truck, did you?" She waited.

A car drove past, the driver aiming a familiar hand gesture at her. He honked the horn while mouthing something behind the closed windows that clearly was not nice. Cassidy ignored the passerby while waiting for Ben's response.

Ben was confused. His head hurt again now that the medicine was out of his system. He twisted in his seat and maneuvered himself to pull up the fabric of his kilt so he could see where a chunk was missing. Damn. He had a big snout shaped, raggedy rip out of the cloth of his kilt. Plus, his truck was dead on the side of the road. Double damn.

Cassidy eased the car to the shoulder of the road, snatched up her phone, and dialed out. Her body was stiff and on point, her features grim. Finally someone answered the other end and she relaxed her shoulders enough to allow her body to rest back into the seat.

"Jon. Thank heavens you answered." She paused, listening. "Yes, well, there's a little glitch in our day. I'm guessing Ben's truck broke down on the side of the road between Murdock's and the office." She looked to Ben for confirmation.

Ben concurred.

"Somehow Ben instinctively went to Knight's for help." She glared at Ben then, letting him see her disapproval while Jon spoke on the other end. "Yeah, well the faster you find that truck and haul it to the office, the more likely Ben will have *any* truck *at all* by the end of the day."

Listening, she paused. "Thank you, Jon. Keep me posted, will you?"

She hit "end" on her phone and slipped it into the bag at her side. "Jon's got this. He'll have the truck returned to your place in a jiffy." She glanced sideways at him before continuing. "After that, we'll see what's what with the engine."

Ben consented. He was glad she knew what to do. She was something else. Smart, too.

"It's a good thing I came looking for you. What the heck were you thinking going to Charlie's for help?" Her forehead scrunched up in irritation. "Don't you know . . .?" The words hung out in the wind. She glanced back at him and visibly wilted. "No, I guess you don't remember." She looked back at the road in front of her. "Sorry. I lost my head there for a minute seeing you running like that."

Ben laughed, without a hint of humor. "Ah guess Ah donae run much either, aye?"

"You run. But it's more. . ." She tilted her head to the side in thought. "It's more controlled. More calculated. Scheduled."

Ben was not amused. "Please, explain that to

47

me, lass. How on God's green earth can a stretch o' the legs in the mornin' sunshine be calculated?"

Cassidy laughed, shaking her head in wonder as a smile grew on her lips. "I don't know, Ben, I can't explain that to myself. You just do. You run maybe three or five days a week. Always at six in the morning, with the proper running gear. You carry two full bottles of water out and come back with two bottles emptied."

Her smile amazed him. "Wha' is proper gear faer running?"

Cassidy lifted a shoulder. "Eh. The usual. T-shirt, wicking of course. Running shorts or pants if it's cold out. Shoes, iPod, whistle."

"Wha' the hell do Ah need a whistle for?"

"You know, it's typical hiking gear. You do that, too. Hike. You lead hiking tours during the warmer seasons." Cassidy slammed down on the steering wheel. "Crappit! I wasn't supposed to tell you any of that!"

Outraged, Ben challenged her. "Why the hell not?"

"Doctor's orders." Cassidy's shoulders drooped. She glanced his way, a frown replacing her happier demeanor. "We're supposed to let you remember on your own, not define life for you. You know?" She reached past the steering wheel to signal her return to the road, glanced in the side mirror for approaching cars, and eased them back into motion. "It's meant to keep you from getting muddled up in the way we think things are or should be in your life."

Ben slouched in his seat as Cassidy turned the car to a street on the left. "I don' need a damn whistle. Ah've been whistlin' on mah own since I was a wee lad barely able t' walk."

Cassidy didn't miss a beat. "Sure you have." She slid a doubtful smile out of the corner of her mouth in his direction.

In turn, Ben puckered his lips and let out a sound that echoed off the interior walls of the car.

Cassidy slammed to a halt smack dab in the middle of the road.

"For the love of . . ." She covered her ears and rubbed. Her eyes were big and her forehead wrinkled in anger. "Please warn me before you *ever* do that again."

A car horn sounded directly behind them.

"Ah guess I donnae usually whistle, then?"

She shook her head, still rubbing her ears. "I can't say I've ever seen or heard you do that before."

Quiet permeated the car.

Ben waved to the car behind them to pass and offered a nod of apology as they drove by. He looked out the side window and let his mind wander back to his earlier thoughts. "D'you wonder why it is, lass, that I can remember how t' drive mah truck but I donnae remember a thing about who Ah 'm or where Ah've come from?"

Cassidy ogled him incredulously, then sighed and relaxed against the back of her own seat. The car continued to idle, her foot on the brake. "Ben," she sighed. "There's no rhyme or reason to what you're remembering and what you're locking away inside your mind. You've been through some trauma. Just give it time. You'll be fine."

"Ah don' even know mah own name, Cassi." His face grew sad. "At least no' that Ah remember, anyway. I only know 'twas written on mah driver's license."

Cassidy smiled at him. She reached over to place her hand on top of his where it lay against his thigh. "You called me Cassi." She squeezed his hand. Tenderness played across her face. "You haven't called me that since second grade."

Ben liked this warmer side of Cassidy, especially the softness of her touch. He turned his hand over and clasped her fingers inside of his own, relishing the feel of them in his grasp. "Wha's second grade?"

Cassidy laughed out loud. "Fair enough," she said, smiling at him and letting him see her kindness as she leaned back into her own seat. "Second grade is a level of school that we attended together, you and I. We were roughly seven years old. It was the year you gave me a piece of red construction paper in the shape of a heart on Valentine's Day. You called me Cassi on the piece of paper."

When she smiled at him he could see it was a cherished and lovely memory, one she obviously held close to her heart.

Cassidy pulled her hand from his grasp and seemed to withdraw deep inside herself by looking away where he couldn't see her face.

"Did Ah say anythin' else to you? On the Valentine?"

She nodded.

"Will y' no' tell me wha' it said, then'?"

Cassidy wiggled in her seat.

Ben perceived she was uncomfortable, so he adjusted his seatbelt and angled his body sideways in order to see her more clearly while he waited for her response.

Cassidy sniffled. She appeared more interested in watching for traffic as she focused her eyes beyond the car, but her actions gave her away as she attempted to wipe her face secretly. Once satisfied with her results, she offered Ben a sideways glance before rolling her eyes in defeat. With no traffic in sight, she put the car back into gear and proceeded forward. Finally, hiding behind her right hand like it was a blinder so he couldn't see her face, she gave him the answer he waited for. "It said in painstakingly beautiful print, 'I love you, my Cassi. Benjamin.'"

Ben comprehended by way of her behavior in the past twenty-four hours that clearly the sentiments of that second grade Valentine's note had never come true in their adult world. "Was tha' the only time Ah've expressed mah feelings t' you, love?"

Cassidy was quiet for several miles, appearing to be lost in an inner battle. Ben didn't press her. For the longest time he sat still, letting her stay away. In the silence, he decided he would make it a point to call her Cassi from then on. Perhaps that bit of tenderness would goad her into staying put when he reached out to touch her now and again. The idea satisfied him and he felt encouraged despite the distance between them at the moment.

Finally, when he was certain she wouldn't answer the question, he excused her. "'Twas a lang time ago."

Cassidy nodded while wiping at another tear threatening to fall. She sniffed and continued down a road he wasn't familiar with, though he could see the river straight ahead.

"Have you been to Skyline?"

"Skyline Mountain Road?"

Cassidy's eyes jumped with excitement. "You remember it then?"

Ben shook his head, sadly. "It's on mah license."

She wilted. They drove on in the quiet sounds

of the road, the whir of wheel to pavement, and an occasional squeak of the front end responding to a dip in the road.

After a few minutes, Ben lost patience with the quiet. "Where were y' goin' when y' saw me on th' side o' the road?"

"I was running a quick errand into Huntsville. I didn't think you'd need me before I got back." Her cheeks glowed red in embarrassment. "I guess I was wrong to think that."

"D' you still need t' go there?"

She nodded, though without much energy. "I do. But Jon's meeting us at the office with your truck soon."

Ben mulled an idea around in his mind. "Can Ah go along for th' ride when you go, Cassi?"

She glanced a wary eye in his direction. "I guess so. Any reason why?"

"Ah believe I've got an errand of my own t' run." Ben smiled and nodded to himself, confirming his own thoughts before sitting back to enjoy the rest of the ride. He draped an arm along the base of the window and relaxed. Yes sir, he had an errand of his own to take care of. And today was the right day to do it.

UPON ARRIVING IN Huntsville, Ben had the forethought to ask Cassidy to drop him off at an intersection near where he needed to go, but far enough as to not give himself away. From there he hiked to the Dodge dealership and proceeded to deal with a salesman for a brand spanking new truck. He'd seen enough evidence on Cassidy's desk that morning to know he had some money. His driver's license assured him he owned some land. And by golly by all that was holy, he needed a new truck. One thing he remembered for certain was that the Dodge Ram was outfitted with a Hemi. And he wanted a Hemi. He could feel it in his soul, God bless him!

But by the time the salesman verified his accounts and handed him the keys, Cassidy was front and center, tapping her toes, arms crossed. The bank had somehow notified her of his purchase and she'd known exactly where to find him.

Ben simply raised an eyebrow back at her and commanded, "You can follow me back t' th' river, Cassi, my love."

The smile he gave her didn't make a dent in her armor, but that little *my love* part he added on made her visibly go soft as a petal. He gave her a wink and they were off, heading back for home, one behind the other.

Once in Riverland, having been allowed time to think, Ben decided the one place he needed to check out more than any other was that address on his driver's license. Maybe it held clues to help him regain his memory. He pulled up to the curb in front of the office and jumped down from his truck to greet Cassidy. She was busy angling her own car next to where Jon, true to his word, had left Ben's dead truck.

Ben, quick to act, was already opening Cassidy's door when she turned off the ignition. "Let's go up t' th' mountain and see wha' we can find, shall we?" He wiggled his eyebrows at her, entreating her to agree.

Cassidy pulled herself out of the car along with the package she'd picked up in the city. She looked up at the sky. "We don't have much daylight left, Ben. Are you sure you don't want to wait and go early tomorrow so you have time to explore the property?"

He scanned the late afternoon sky. A bank of clouds loomed on the horizon. "How long does it take to drive there?"

"Oh, not long. Twenty minutes or so? But you won't have a lot of time to scout it out. Maybe a half hour, if that."

"A half hour is long enough to ge' mah first glimpse o' it." He paused in thought before nodding his certainty that they did in fact have enough time. "Ah'm jus' curious t' see it. Maybe it holds a clue or two for my mem'ry banks."

"Well then, let me put these things in the office and we'll get going."

Cassidy did as planned, but when she met him at the truck, a funny thing happened. Ben opened the door for her to climb in and, well, she was short. Too short. So she busied herself by placing a knee on the floorboard of the truck and was preparing to lift herself up into the cab by holding onto the seatbelt when Ben saw his opportunity.

"Oh no you don', lass. Ah canno' ha' you fallin' out o' my truck before you've ev'n got inside it." He pushed an arm under her knees and pulled her back to fall into his chest.

Cassidy squealed. "You can't pick me up Ben! Your head!"

"Aye lass, but Ah can and Ah did." He wiggled his eyebrows playfully. "Pu' your arm aroun' mah neck, love. Ah'll lift you into your seat."

When Cassidy followed his instructions, Ben felt the need to protect her, to reel her in, to claim her. He wanted to keep her close, tight, for himself.

"We won't be able to see your land well if you don't put me in that truck and get us driving down the road, Ben." She dropped her head to the side, questioning him.

"Right, A'm driving us t' th' mountain." Lordy, but she was a beautiful creature, even more so in his arms.

"Only if you put me in the truck and get

yourself buckled in, too."

He let his eyes fall to her mouth. Need roared to life inside him. He considered briefly what would happen if he carried her off to his room. Her tongue eased out and licked her top lip. His body responded in turn, involuntarily pushing a low growl from deep inside his chest. Her tongue captivated him. She ran it across the pink planes of her lower lip before pulling it back inside. "You're drivin' me ou' o' my min' with your mouth, Cassi."

Her eyes grew big in response as she watched what he would do. Finally, she pushed against his shoulders emphatically. "Get with the program, Ben. You bought this truck. Let's see what it can do!"

# CHAPTER FIVE

BEN DROVE, WITH the help of Cassidy's directions, up the mountain to his Skyline Mountain Road property. Clouds bumped into the higher elevated landscape and brought a colder bite to the air. The drab colors of the sky washed everything in gloom and sadness. The water that leaked from the rocks lining the mountain road looked thicker here, indicating a potential freeze in the near future.

Cassidy sat on the far side of the cab, lost in managerial tasks, texting and amending a reservation with guests due to arrive later that month. For Ben, the trek up the curving, winding roads gave him time and opportunity to think.

As the miles passed by, the distance between homes grew. Some were old and well maintained, others seemed to beg the earth to swallow them whole, to put an end to their misery. Ben wondered, what was his own house like? Old, new, or somewhere in between? Fresh and clean, refurbished, what? But only one question remained upon their arrival. Why was Skyline Mountain Road listed as his place of residence on his driver's license when all that remained was a mailbox and a panoramic view of sky, land, and valley below?

Trees creaked and moaned their discontent with the cold as Ben and Cassidy exited the truck. Cassidy didn't waste any time and took off for the edge of the property. Ben was grateful for the distance she gave him to take it all in.

He breathed in deeply and let his eyes scan the area. Bugger, but this was an empty place. It looked like a nice enough piece of land, though abandoned to the elements. But for what reason? A section of earth was scratched out where a house once stood. In the center of the area facing the road was a dip in the dirt, obviously worn from use. Probably where the front steps were previously located if the crepe myrtle tree, gnarled with vines, was any witness. Neglect is what that poor tree signified and it stabbed at his heart.

When Ben approached the place where the back of the house once stood, he noticed Cassidy angling herself over the low-lying stone wall that lined the rear of the property. When positioned on the other side, she eased down onto the hard surface and sat, looking out over the landscape beyond. Ben turned around to scan the width of the property. It was a good piece of land, but it needed tending. Barren kudzu vines coiled willy-nilly, a true sign of trouble. But if it was cleaned up, it could be something. Maybe it could be the place for a new house. A new home. A new family.

Ben looked back to where Cassidy sat studying the valley below. He ambled over and took a seat straddling the wall near her. Cassidy shuddered in the cold. Ben followed her eyes and marveled at the million-dollar view.

"It's a fine place for a home."

Cassidy turned to him, smiled sadly. "It's the best view Skyline has to offer."

"Why's that?"

"You can see the peak of Skyline better than anyone around." Cassidy aimed her head in the direction of where someone was working on the Skyline Christmas sign. She pulled a hand out of her pocket to point down past the naked trees that filled the mountainside. "You can see all of Riverland as easily, too. It's the best of both worlds." She pushed her hand back into her pocket and visibly shivered.

Ben nodded and focused his attention back at the space between him and the road. "There was a house at one time."

"Yes, there was a house."

He looked at her then, eye to eye. "Tell me

what you know of the house, Cassi. Was it a house full of happiness?"

"I don't know. It was empty after your grandfather died. You had it bulldozed two years ago."

"Why's that?"

"Your truck couldn't make it up here in bad weather so you couldn't live here. And besides, it was kind of falling apart at the seams. Dangerous even. Too many broken windows and sagging boards. The roof was starting to fall in. Someone was bound to get hurt, you said."

Sadness threaded through her words. Ben saw the full picture she painted and made a sound of acknowledgment.

"You don't recall any of it?"

Ben aimed his head in the direction of where the house would've been. Hope jumped in his chest reaching for something to jump-start his memory. "No' e'en a bit."

Cassidy sighed and stood to walk away. "I'm cold. I need to move and warm up." The wind gusted and made her lose her balance. Ben caught her, catching her off guard, and pulled her into his lap, wrapping her in his arms as he did so.

"Sorry." Embarrassment colored her face with red.

Ben grinned wickedly. "Sorry is th' last thing Ah'm, lass."

He moved her hair away from her eyes. The wind wreaked havoc on it, whipping it around her head here and there. Cassidy pushed her face into his hand at the first touch of his warmth.

"Oh, you are so warm. Both hands please."

Ben extended his other hand and enveloped her face in his heat.

She sighed her contentment.

As Ben held her face and watched her nestling into his grasp, he was drawn into her softness again, her gentleness, her lack of gall. She was so fair and lovely. Her eyes fluttered open. She smiled up at him as he closed the distance between them. She sucked in a breath of surprise as he touched her lips with his own, testing, then teasing. Cassidy didn't return his explorations right away, but she didn't run. He leaned back to study her eyes. Something in them showed her fear but she held still in his hands.

He ran a thumb across her bottom lip. "Ah want t' know you, Cassi. Ah want t' remember who y'are t' me, love. Ah'd like t' think we're good toge'er, you and Ah."

Cassidy began shaking her head but he stilled her.

"Wha'ever was before, le' us forget jus' now." Ben touched her then, again easing himself across her lips. And when he heard her sigh and felt her lean slightly forward, he pulled her closer and took to her mouth like a starving man.

Cassidy's hands slipped up his chest and beyond, wrapping around his neck. Ben eased his hands down to her hips to pull her tight, letting her feel his response. His tongue danced around hers. He breathed in her scent and took the fleshy softness of her backside into his hands and squeezed. Cassidy moaned. Ben continued laving her mouth and allowed his body to direct them. He stood and lifted his leg over the wall, backed them up together against the hard cold surface, and as he eased down to sit again, he pushed her legs to either side, wrapping her body to straddle his own.

Cassidy tried to complain, but he shushed her with further kisses across her cheeks as he traveled around to nip at her neck, whispering senseless words along the way. Words of pleasure and praise, entreaties of openings and takings. Holding her steady with one hand, he let the other roam to weigh her breast. He squeezed gently, looking back into her eyes, watching for approval. She appeared lost in pleasure as he slipped a thumb across her hard nipple, provoking it to reach for his mouth. "Aye, tha' you were wearin' skirts, Ah'd be in y' already, givin' you mah full hilt, lass."

Cassidy gasped then. Ben took her nipple into his mouth through her clothes and tugged, gently scraping his teeth across it as he receded back. Cassidy's hand gripped his shoulders and then she gave him a push.

"You want me to stop, lass?"

Dazed and confused, Cassidy came back to the present quickly. She leapt off his lap. "Oh God. No! Sorry. I mean yes! Yes. Stop." She frantically brushed her hands at her flyaway hair, busied herself with zipping her jacket, closing herself off from him.

"Aye, now lassie. There's no need t' be like tha'."

"Like what?"

Not for the first time Ben watched her face flush before she reeled in her emotions, spun to leap over the wall, and marched towards the truck with her back up straight.

Ben sighed. *There she goes again. Running away from me.* He looked over his shoulder to see her hips swaying to the beat of his blood, making him laugh out loud. "Aye, now tha's th' way of i'. You tease me ye' again."

After walking around the mountaintop, measuring and imagining, Ben settled Cassidy in the passenger side of the truck before entering on the driver's side. The heat was warm pushing past the vents into their faces. He sat looking out across the valley one last time, lost in thought. Cassidy waited at his side patiently, warming her hands in the heat the truck offered, her feet dangling from the seat, too short for reaching the floorboards.

"I remember my Mam-maw used to stand at a

window overlooking that view there." He nodded to himself, absorbed by the memory. "She would wash dishes and sing hymns through the open window to anything beyond its panes that would listen. Paw-paw would stand in the hallway door and watch her without letting on he was nearby. When she would finish the song she'd tell him thank you for listening. He'd applaud her before taking her into his arms for a spin around the kitchen floor. She would laugh." He paused. Sadness sat on his shoulders. "God, I'll never forget the sound of her laughter. She was so beautiful the way she laughed at his carryings on." Ben turned and looked at Cassidy watching him. "Mah gran'parents were amazing people, weren't they, lass." It wasn't a question, but rather a statement of fact.

Cassidy nodded in agreement, letting him remember the good times. "Yes. They were amazing."

Ben slipped the truck into gear. "Tha's all Ah remember."

"No. I don't think so." Cassidy looked strange. Confounded, even.

"No? Wha' d' you mean, love?"

"You remembered to speak in plain English. No brogue."

"Aye. Ah suppose Ah did do that."

They headed back down the side of the mountain together, hope invading past the mountainside all the way into the cab of the truck.

WHEN MORNING BROKE for Cassidy the next day (around the time a rooster rolls over and pulls his blanket back up over his head) she hit the finance books and stock exchange reports, desperate to find a way to cover for the expense of a brand new Dodge Ram 3500 Hemi. She didn't much care that it could lift the Titanic out of the river or haul a trailer house to some park nearby. She didn't even care that it could make it up the mountain in the aftermath of an ice storm. She wouldn't be around to see any of that if Ben came back into his right mind and found that she had let him spend umpteen-bazillion-dollars on a truck he never would've bought in his wildest dreams. No siree, she wasn't going to live to tell her grandkids because he would kill her on the spot if he ever found out she was the one who had Power of Attorney when he bought that ginormous truck currently sitting in the driveway. Right next to the one he loved. The one that cost him pennies to repair on any given day. Without the help of Charlie Knight. The one his grandfather had given him along with his first driver's license way too many years ago.

By eight that morning she was on coffee pot number two with a solution in sight when Ben walked into the office and stretched all his kilted wares out in front of her to see. God but he was a handsome devil, which was why she ignored him completely.

Ben pouted.

The landline rang and after answering, Cassidy handed the phone to Ben, still focused on the numbers of her plan. "It's for you."

Ben took the phone from her. "G'morning."

Someone on the other end spoke.

Ben looked puzzled. "Th' return is two days late, y' say?"

Again a pause for someone to respond. In detail, apparently.

Concern began to spike Ben's words. "Th' jackets, vests, and accessories were returned t' your store wi'out the kilts three days ago?"

Cassidy looked up from her computer screen, on full alert.

Ben placed a hand over the phone, hiding his words from the caller. Tension bunched his forehead. "Di' y' know the kilts were rentals, love?"

"Oh. That." Cassidy pushed her chair back and then stood to walk around the desk. She took the phone from him and shooed him off toward the coffee pot. "Go! I've got this."

She gave him another nod of the head to

encourage him. Ben walked away questioning her, so she turned her back to him, lowering her voice so he couldn't hear her end of the conversation.

"Hello. This is Cassidy Spencer, Mr. Murray's business manager. I'm really very sorry, but I'm going to have to apologize. There's been a little bit of a hiccup." She paused, then laughed nervously. She angled her head to eye Ben and verify that he couldn't hear her.

Ben was manning a hot cup of coffee and his attention was fixed on something beyond her view outside the window.

"Mr. Murray suffered a little bit of an accident that caused him to lose his memory. And well, umm, he kind of sort of thought he owned those kilts?"

Silence.

Cassidy's head bobbed up and down, affirming whatever was said on the other end of the line. "Yes ma'am, that's exactly right. He has forgotten everything. Well, mostly everything." Hopefully, the rental agent understood the dilemma entirely. "And I didn't realize someone else had already returned part of the order to you." Cassidy laughed nervously before continuing. "Sorry, it's been a little crazy, what with his memory and all."

Ben walked past her towards the supply room and quietly mouthed "Aunt Patty returned a few things the day after New Year's before I could stop her."

"If he has *forgotten,* then I'm sure two hundred and five dollars A DAY rental fee for EACH suit will help him remember *just fine!"*

Ben directed a raised eye at Cassidy as the yelling came through the wires loud and clear.

Cassidy held the phone away from her ear, jerking as the last few words shrilled loudly. She cautiously replaced the receiver back to her ear to respond. "I will handle this right away."

The voice on the other end continued in loud form. "I have another wedding party waiting in line for those kilts so until the entire order is returned, the *entire* price is in effect for *each and every day!"*

"Yes sir. I mean, ma'am. I understand." Cassidy remembered the kilt Ben was wearing when he had been attacked by Charlie's dog. "Out of curiosity, how much would it be to purchase one of the kilts?"

The response that came through the lines may as well have presented the woman in person for all the presence it brought into the room with its voluminous shout. *"Those kilts are NOT for sale!"*

"Yes ma'am! I understand clearly." Cassidy stood at attention, holding back a ridiculous need to salute. "I'll have them back to you within the hour, sir. I mean ma'am. Sir." She jerked as an exploding sound rang from the earpiece announcing a disconnect on the other end.

"Well." She eyed the phone before gently replacing it to its rest.

Ben stood undaunted, watching for her response.

Cassidy mirrored his demeanor, quietly trying to construct an explanation. She busied her hands with tracing the outline of the phone's earpiece as she thought.

"So my cousin's wedding went off without a hitch, then?"

Cassidy jerked her head up to look him in the eye.

"It's all right, Cass. I remember standing up for them on New Year's Day, ringing in the year with two hundred other witnesses."

"You do?"

"Yes," he nodded. "Did the bride's family make it back t' Scotland okay?"

Cassidy agreed quietly. Clearly his brogue was slipping away.

Ben walked back to the window and sighed. "I seem t' remember you weren't there, Cass. Why's that?"

Cassidy's stomach hurt. He'd fallen back into calling her Cass like all the other locals. Her heart squeezed inside her chest. She circled the desk and sat down behind it, placing her head in her hands, hiding from him in case he turned back around. "I'm sorry, Ben. I just couldn't."

"You weren't secretly pining for my cousin or anything, were you?"

"No. I'm not *pining away* over your cousin." She wanted to bang her head on the wood surface but she couldn't do that anymore than she could look into Ben's mossy eyes and tell him she was *pining* away for him. *Lordy but would this torturous love in her heart ever end?*

Ben threw back the last of his coffee. "Well, I guess that solves the mystery of the bridal company on caller ID!"

Cassidy swung her head up in response. "Wait. You've been checking our calls?"

Ben grunted. "It's business, Cass. You checked for numbers, too, right?"

"Well, yes, but. . ."

Ben reached over to ruffle her hair like he'd done a million times throughout her life. "It's okay. It's what we do around here to check for missed reservation calls, right?" He chuckled then winked at her before turning to leave. "I'm going to go drive my new truck and fit it out with my supplies and such." He stopped short of the door and turned back to face her. "You wouldn't happen to know what happened to my cell phone, would you?"

Cassidy recovered it from the desk drawer and laid it on top for him to examine. "It's dead though. I don't know where your charger is."

Ben stepped back to the desk and pocketed his

phone. "Now *that*, I do know. It's in my old truck. I just didn't know what it went to until now." And with that he waved off as if nothing was out of the ordinary in their world.

Cassidy looked back at the computer monitor and determined it was time to make some money, and *fast. Risks be damned!*

# CHAPTER SIX

BEN PRIED CASSIDY out of the office approximately an hour after the sun went down, promising her a surprise made in heaven, a picnic on the mountain underneath the stars. In the warmth of his truck, of course. The clouds had moved past late in the afternoon but they left a bone-piercing cold in their wake. But he'd come through for her honestly, she thought, as she bit into the best bite of barbeque the south had to offer. Straight from Henry's kitchen. Ben supplied her with a side of beans and potato salad, too, and a pickle sitting on top of her pulled pork exactly how she liked it. That he'd remembered the pickle made her feel all warm and fuzzy inside. Things were looking up.

On that note, she internally patted herself on the back for the quick investment turnaround she'd made earlier in the day. At ten that morning she'd bought, by three in the afternoon she'd sold, and doubled half of Ben's liquid assets, more than making up for his shopping spree. Not bad for a day full of number playing. Not bad at all. Best of all, he'd never miss a dime for spending it on that fancy new truck they were sitting in, either, since she'd also paid off the loan he'd taken out.

"It's a little warm in here for my comfort level. Would you like to join me under the stars in the bed of the truck?" He wiggled his eyebrows at her suggestively. "I've got plenty of blankets to keep you warm."

Cassidy laughed at him. "Is that what you meant when you said you left to stock your truck this morning?" She goosed him in his side, riling and teasing him. "You're such a man!"

"I don't know what you're talking about!" Ben feigned ignorance, grinning wickedly. "I'm merely offering a front row seat showcasing the heavenly expanse."

"Pshaw! You've never been a good liar, Ben Murray! There's no sense starting that business now." She grinned, shaking her head at him in fun.

They climbed down out of the cab of the truck. Ben helped her into the back where he revealed a masterfully planned layout of blankets, pillows, and comfort for stargazing. Once she was comfortable against the pillow-lined cab of the truck, Ben settled in next to her and pulled her close. They sat in silence for the longest time, watching, waiting for the heavens to move. The stars were in full regalia for the evening, the cold atmosphere showcasing them in their diamond bright brilliance.

Cassidy didn't know what to do with herself. Sure, she'd been this close to Ben before, especially so in the past few days, though usually it was more of a brother–sister occasion. But their world was new and unproven now, unknown. It was shaky and risky and uncertain, unlike the numbers she'd spent her day with. Numbers were reliable. Love was not. This situation didn't make her feel altogether safe. She knew firsthand that tomorrow could bring an entirely new set of circumstances, likely the very same problems she tried to run away from only three days ago. She wasn't kidding herself. She did love Ben. Yes, she loved him with all her heart. In fact, she couldn't remember what it was like *not* to love Ben Murray. He may not have intentionally returned her love, except for that one little Valentine's Day paper heart with the handwriting of a young boy, but he was always up in the big middle of her life for every joy, celebration, and even the unfortunate events of life. He was there for her whether he wanted to admit it or not. But she wanted more. No, that wasn't true. She *needed* more. She *needed* to be loved and adored openly and for all to see. She *needed* to be praised and relished in every way by her man.

Cassidy redirected her attention back to Ben who was intent on watching the sky, certain he'd spot a meteor in the cold Alabama night. His mind was void of any memory of her shortcomings or long suits and he'd somehow lost years of data on her. But something existed, safely tucked away inside his mind, something enough to drive him to pull her close in this little disturbance of his life. She was glad to be there with him.

Cassidy snuggled in closer to Ben's side and shivered.

"Are you warm enough?" He looked down into her eyes as he eased the blanket tighter around her shoulders. His gaze dipped to watch as she ran her tongue across her lips.

"I'm okay so long as you keep me close." She smiled.

Ben reached and smoothed a hand across her face, holding her cheek in its warmth. "I'll keep you warm, Cassi." He bent his face to hers, paused, and touched her lips with his own softly. He leaned back enough for words to escape him, and whispered to her and the whole universe, "I promise."

With those two words, Cassidy lost all inhibition and pushed herself forward to take anything and everything Ben Murray could give her this cold winter's night. Because it could be that *this* night was the only time she would ever have her man. Without Ben, her life was empty and colder than anything the world could offer her. Should tomorrow come and Ben walk away from her for the remembering, then she would at least have tonight. She would have given her all. She would move forward either way.

BEN COLLAPSED ON top of Cassi, breathing heavily, trying desperately to make his chest calm down to a reasonable rhythm. He couldn't remember ever being so entirely satiated than he was in this moment with Cassi under the stars. He rolled away from her without letting go such that she stayed wrapped together with him. Ben draped an arm over his head and counted his breathing to help it steady. When he could finally find his voice, he asked, "Are you okay?"

Cassidy didn't say a word, she merely nudged his shoulder and let her arm rest across his chest in a heap of exhaustion.

"I didn't hurt you, did I?" Ben squeezed her, forcing her to look into his face for him to see for himself. He scanned her eyes, her mouth. "Never in my life would I want to hurt you, Cassi."

A single tear ran down Cassidy's face, catching the light of the stars above.

Ben caught the droplet on his fingertip, puzzled

and a little bit alarmed. "Why are you crying?"

Again, she didn't say anything but rather lifted her shoulder in uncertainty. Their eyes caught and both understood instinctively what the other felt. There were simply too many unknowns. Too much uncertainty.

Ben pulled her head back to lay on his shoulder and sighed. They peered into the night empty of the world and hoping for the heavens to declare their mission, their purpose. High above them, in the expanse of the sky, a light shot across the entire blanket of night for them both to witness.

Ben squeezed Cassidy tight. "See. There's something spectacular waiting for us up ahead." He looked at her again. "Something special for you and me. Together, Cassidy. I think we were meant to be in this place together." He pointed upwards. "The sky agrees." He smiled, looking back at her, then nodded as if saying, *it is so*.

Cassidy hadn't agreed with him, but she hadn't disagreed, either. Ben let that settle over him and laid still for what seemed an eternity, imagining what it could be like to have Cassidy wrapped up in his life forever. When he heard her breathing settle in for the night, he simply followed her to dreamland on top of his mountain. He let his mind take charge casting his future for a little while. The sun would come up tomorrow soon enough. Then he'd make some real decisions.

# CHAPTER SEVEN

BEN PULLED UP to the edge of the wall at his property on Skyline Mountain Road mid-morning. He'd settled Cassidy back in at the office earlier, before the light of day had opportunity to appear. She'd been quiet, but seemed pleasant after the night's events. Ben aimed his new truck in the direction of the sky at the stone wall's edge. Bolton Matthews, a childhood friend who'd been too busy in his own life to stay in touch, pulled right alongside of him, and then jumped out to greet him like old friends.

"Man! I never would've thought this day would happen." Bolton slapped a hand into Ben's, shaking it vigorously.

Ben, a bit confused, shook back. "Why's that?"

Bolton slipped his hand into his pocket for warmth and resumed an easy stance. "Well, you know. It's been a long time, is all."

Ben let it go at face value and concentrated on his reason for calling Bolton to the mountaintop. "So, I'm wondering what it would cost me to build a new home on this spot. Something like my grandparents' old home, but updated with modern conveniences. Do you think you can spec it out and give me an estimate?"

"Sure, I can." Bolton smiled with relief lacing the edges of his face. "It *is* my business after all." He chuckled. "Tell me what you want and I'll calculate what I can do pricewise. How does that sound?"

The two of them put their heads together over the blueprints Ben provided of his grandparents' old home. They spent the following hour walking the position of the structure on the land itself. They took some measurements, threw out ideas between them, mulling over possibilities but maintaining the concept of the original home. About the time they were sitting on the tailgate of the truck, talking textiles and finishes, Jon and Cassidy arrived in her car, both looking pretty worried. Bear pulled in right behind them in his old beater truck, dressed for business.

"Hey guys! What's up?" Ben hopped off the gate and hustled to greet them. Bolton held back, waiting for the dust to settle with the new arrivals.

Jon slapped Ben's shoulder in a brotherly not-so-close-but-close-enough-hug, all the while aiming a watchful eye in Bolton's direction. "Bolton." He spoke low and motioned his head in recognition of the other man's attendance.

Bear, not so eloquent, stood with feet rooted to the ground, knees slightly bent, hands lightly splayed on hips ready for a fight. "What the hell's going on here?"

Cassidy looked like she wanted to be anywhere but on that particular mountain.

Ben aimed his attention at Cassidy. "Is everything okay, Cassi?"

Both Jon and Bear let no time pass before pushing past Ben, proceeding straight to Bolton, hackles up, ready to take him down.

"What the hell, guys?" Ben followed, confusion quickly turning to anger.

Jon pushed Bolton's shoulder. "What are you up to, Bolton?" He waited ten seconds, then blazed forward. Jon's jaw twitched like it always did right before he lost all control. "Did you think because you found me a deal on some reclaimed floors you could win our good graces? Huh? You think you've paid for your sins now? Or are you trying to take advantage of Ben while he's down, huh?"

Ben pushed between the two men, forcing some space between them. "What do you mean take advantage of me? I asked Bolton to meet me here to talk business, man! Back off!"

Bear stood three feet away, his emotions barely in check, ready to pounce if given half a chance.

Ben gave Bear the evil eye. "You too, man." He held Bear's attention without flinching. "Cassidy. Explain."

Cassidy stepped up to his side and pleaded with him. "Ben, we were alarmed. We don't want you doing anything you might regret later, is all."

"Regret? You think I would regret building a modern version of my grandparents' home here on this mountain?" Ben was completely confused by what was happening. "Why would I regret that, Cassidy?"

Before Cassidy could respond, Bear leapt. "I'll tell you why you'd regret it. This lowlife doesn't deserve to spit on your shoes much less rebuild your home after what he's done."

"What has he done?" Ben's voice was beginning to rise with frustration.

Bear gave Bolton a direct shove towards the wall, backing it up with his whole body shoving harder.

Jon was right there with him. Side by side, Bear and Jon were forcing Bolton backwards, dangerously close to the edge of the drop-off.

"Let them deal with this, Ben." Cassidy tugged at Ben's sleeve. She pleaded with him with her eyes. "They know what they're doing. Bolton, too. Come with me and let them be."

Ben's irritation skyrocketed. He was sick and tired of his friends trying to "handle" him. He wasn't stupid. He knew they'd been withholding information from him so he had time to regain his own memories. But picking a fight with a man that had done nothing to hurt anyone else was wrong. He set Cassidy aside, told her to let him handle his own fight, and then off he went to push his friends each into their own corners so they could all work out this misunderstanding like grown-ass adults. But when he stepped into the mix, fists flew. He pushed himself into the fray as Jon's fist aimed for Bolton's face, and, slamming into Ben instead, pummeled him toward the ground. The wall between it and him jutted out a fraction, enough to catch his head before he could find the earth. Ben's head hit the stone. He wilted from there, hitting the cold hard dirt with a thud.

A loud gasp invaded the air as Cassidy watched the whole testosterone-laden episode play out in front of her. All three men left standing stood watching in horror as Ben splayed across the cold dirt of the mountain. Time hung between them all, counting off the hour-long seconds once again, giving them each time to sort out their own reactions.

Cassidy landed on Ben first, checking for a pulse, for blood, for some semblance of life. Tears ran in rivers down her cheeks. Her nose dripped and she wiped unconsciously at it with the sleeve of her jacket. Her hands trembled as she ran them over the new injuries of his head.

Bear and Bolton were shouting overhead about girlfriends, babies, and some crazy nonsense. Jon crouched down next to Ben's side, waiting for Cassidy's orders.

Ben groaned. *Holy son of a . . . good gracious molly*! *Damn but my head hurts.* He reached up to touch his head, pulled back to inspect his fingers. No blood. Cassidy insistently prodded him, wanting to know how many fingers she was holding up. Jon bellowed out orders saying someone needed to call 911. Ben could barely make out a pair of work boots shuffling on the side with some brown oxfords, dirt flying all around the scuffle with words meant only for a late-night bar crowd to hear. He lifted himself up on his hands and knees and dragged in a deep breath. Maybe if he could breathe in and out he could stand up. He tried. He wavered back down. Jon caught him.

"Catch your breath, man. Sit still and catch your breath." Jon held Ben in place so he couldn't do anything but breathe, take in the details. He rolled his head to find Cassidy on his other side. Her tear-covered face said it all. She was scared to death. *But why?*

That's when the pieces all came together inside his brain like they were made of magnets clinging to each other to make sense of his life. Dicker's Christmas lights. The ladder. The emergency room at the hospital. Charlie Knight and his dog. His new truck. The star-lit night. Cassidy open to him, bare as the day she was born, and offering her body to him for pleasure and safekeeping. The wedding rings he'd taken out of the drawer this morning for the purpose of asking Cassidy to be his wife. They were his grandparents' wedding rings left to him for claiming his own love. Which was why he'd come up here together with Bolton on a whim and imagineered a modified family home for Cassidy from the prints left behind of the original Murray home on this very mountain plot. Bolton, the rat-snake who'd run off with another girl at the end of high school and left Bear's sister, Angel, heartbroken after an entire lifetime of planning to marry her and spend the rest of their lives together. A wash of nausea ran through his body and Ben felt like he was going to throw up. He closed his eyes and willed himself to pull it together.

Cassidy spoke softly to him. She smoothed her hand over his sleeve, reminding him she was on his side. "Ben, what can I do for you? What can we all do to help you?"

Ben sat back on his haunches, still taking in controlled breaths. He pinched the bridge of his nose, then followed up by wiping his cold, wind-chapped face with his hand, essentially pushing all of the day's complications away. Then he stood, with Jon's assistance, balanced himself, and braced his hands on his hips.

Bolton and Bear were twenty yards away still thrashing in the dirt, scraping out the past from each other's hides.

Jon watched Ben, ready to jump to his aid at the slightest indication of distress. Cassidy cried the worst kind of tears, silent tears. Painful tears. The kind of tears that ripped your soul apart while you're holding someone else together.

Ben turned and stretched one foot towards the road, set it in place and followed with the other foot, careful to stabilize himself before standing still. He took a deep breath, encouraged by his success so far. "I like the truck, by the way." He looked at Cassidy. "You like it, too, right?"

She nodded carefully.

Ben smiled at her, trying his damnedest to tell her everything would be all right.

She hesitantly smiled back.

"It'll maneuver this mountain easily enough, all the way through the winter months."

Ben opened his arms wide for his *Cassi*, and without delay, she stepped in, right where he wanted her to be. He rested his head on hers and spoke in a thick brogue tongue. "Cassi, for th' love o' all things holy, please won' y' make all mah dreams come true?"

Cassidy jerked back in shock to look into his face. "That's what you said to me that first night in the storeroom!"

"Aye, lass, I did."

She searched his eyes for mockery. "Are you sure you meant it?"

"When, love? Then or now?"

"Both." Her forehead wrinkled in worry. Her eyes dropped down and she fiddled with a button on his shirt. "You can't say something like that to me, Ben Murray."

"Why not, Cassi?" His smile reached out to her through the words, an attempt to pull her eyes back to his.

"Because." Cassidy looked away towards Ben's truck, a reminder of what they had been together, no doubt.

Ben followed her gaze. "Last night I loved you with all I had to give. And today I love you more, Cassi." Ben dropped down on one knee, failed, and ended up on two knees with both Jon and Cassidy trying to catch him. He brushed them off. "It's good. I'm good." He took Cassidy's hand into his and looked back up at her from bended knee. "This morning I took out a velvet box my grandfather gave to me and decided I would do something with it today."

She appeared to consider his words, watching him as she spoke. "I'm not sure I understand where you're going with this, Ben."

He drew in a long, deep breath of air, looked to Jon, and exhaled. Bear and Bolton were laying on the ground, moaning. He turned back to face her. "I mean to ask you to be my wife, Cassidy Spencer."

Cassidy gasped as she brought one hand to her throat. "You what?" New tears began to form and fall.

Ben nodded. "I love you more now than I ever could've in second grade. I've been too much a fool to say so. If you'll have my stubborn arse, I'd like for you to be my wife, to have my babies, and grow old together with me on this enduring mountain."

Jon pumped a fist into the air and shouted with joy, then started texting at the speed of light so all their family and friends were clued in.

Bolton and Bear groaned in harmony, "It's about damn time." They looked at each other, there in the dirt, and agreed. "Idiot!"

Cassidy's hands covered her mouth. Her head moved from side to side, slowly in disbelief.

Ben smiled, hopeful. "Does this mean yes, you will? No, you can't believe I'm finally coming to my senses?" Concern leaked into his eyes before continuing on. "Or is it a no, you won't take my hand in marriage? Please put me out of my misery, lass. Give me an answer to my question?"

Cassidy threw her arms around his shoulders and kissed the top of his head. "Yes, you big

Scottish brogey! Yes! I would love to be your wife!"

Ben gingerly stood and then embraced the love of his life. "I will love you forever, Cassidy soon-to-be-Murray. Always and forever, I am yours." His eyes gleamed down at her. "I promise."

He set his lips to hers, sealed his love that very moment, letting her know he remembered all of her from the night before underneath the star-filled expanse. When Bear finally ambled himself over to join in the congratulations, Ben pulled back and commanded the men. "All this business about Bolton is over. *Finito.* Angel's a big girl, she can fend for herself."

Bear reluctantly agreed after a moment of consideration.

"Besides, I hear he's got his due." Jon piped up with a grin.

"What's that?" Bear asked.

Bolton painfully staggered into the mix. "I've got myself two kids and no wife. She left after running up all of my credit cards and emptying my bank accounts. I can barely order supplies for construction jobs."

"No kidding." Bear crossed his arms and glared at the man in question. "Karma and all that. Rough woman, that one."

"Speaking of money," Ben aimed at Cassidy.

As quick as possible, Cassidy escaped Ben and

took off at a full run. "You can't pin me with anything!" she yelled over her shoulder. When she'd put the truck between them, she added, "Besides, I doubled your assets yesterday! You're in better shape than ever and now you have a new truck that actually runs, too!"

The men all joined in and agreed with her.

Ben smiled and wondered at his good fortune.

"What's that stupid smile on your face for, Scotty?" Bear asked.

Ben angled his head in thought before answering. "Why did it take me so long to do anything about Cassidy, anyway?"

Jon answered without delay. "Your grandfather put the idea in your head that women weren't worth their trouble when your grandmother died."

"Why ever not?"

"Because she died on him, I guess?"

Ben shook his head in disbelief. "But she was seventy-four years old when she died."

"That's the pisser, man! They had a good long life together!"

"I don't understand." Ben was clearly out of the loop of what his grandfather's complaining centered around.

"She left him, Ben. It made him mad that she died. So in his grief he said they weren't worth the trouble."

"That's the dumbest thing I've ever heard!"

The three men rolled their eyes at Ben.

"I know, right?" Jon slapped him on the back. "It's about time you got it, my man."

"Why didn't somebody tell me?"

Everyone, Cassidy included, started stepping all over their words explaining in great detail how stubborn he really was.

FIVE WEEKS LATER, the soonest Ben could rent a kilt and run down some Scottish thistle and heather, Benjamin Thomas Murray carried his woman, his one and only Valentine, Cassidy Murray over the threshold at The River Rat Boat Rentals and Cottages, Cottage No. 7, the honeymoon suite.

Everyone they loved was in attendance at their wedding. Mama Paula gushed over Ben behind the scenes, making sure he had the right jacket and accessories, plus an appropriate gift for Cassidy. She'd even given him a mother–son talk in the absence of his own mother. Bear grumbled about it, but he booked a flight back from Italy for the big event. He'd said that seeing his own woman, Julia, made up for the hardship. Jon, Christy, and Rudi, along with Bolton and his two children celebrated the day together with them, too. Even Dicker made an appearance in the far corners of the chapel. Four of Bear's sisters surrounded Angel on the third row of the groom's side. Mama Paula's pride shone for all the world to see. Her five daughters and one son were all together for the day supporting their friends wholeheartedly. Henry insisted on catering since he'd been in the middle of the Scottish charade that brought Ben and Cassidy together. He told her parents, who flew in from some place up north, that it was the least he could do for Cassidy since she saved his business from being torn apart by the likes of a Scot. One of the Murdock sisters caught the bouquet, but Ben's money was on Bolton being the next to marry after catching the garter belt, what with the exchange he saw between Bolton and Angel when no one was looking. Sadly, no one saw Charlie Knight in the mix. But that was to be expected until Ben let the poor man work on his new truck someday. The best part of the reception was when Christy's water broke. Once again, his friends all rushed to the hospital to greet a new member of their heart-filled southern family.

And so Benjamin and Cassidy Murray lived happily ever after. Of course, Ben handed over all of his money for Cassidy to multiply with her fancy investment skills, which precipitated a vastly better life. And that was a good thing, since he planned on having a whole mess of kids for them to spoil rotten with their love.

### Thank you, readers!

I am grateful to you for taking the time to purchase and read REMEMBERING SKYLINE. If you enjoyed this book, please leave a review at any retailer or on Goodreads.

I love hearing from readers and fans! Please stay in touch with me via the links below. And be sure to watch for more titles coming your way very soon.

Facebook: Lesia Flynn Author Page
Twitter: @LesiaFlynn
Website: www.LesiaFlynn.com

# Coming Soon!

**The last book in the Skyline Mountain Series**

# *SKYLINE RESCUE*

*featuring Bolton and Angel.*

*You won't want to miss their story of putting*

*the past behind*

*and rediscovering who they really are.*

# ABOUT THE AUTHOR

Lesia Flynn is a native of Louisiana. She studied graphic design at LA Tech University. She lives in northern Alabama with her husband, children, and a rescue cat who is determined to save her from life's daily mishaps. She enjoys reading, writing, music, and art, but most of all, anything that provides an adventure! She loves hearing from fans. Please visit www.LesiaFlynn.com to connect with her.